D1572886

ABDO Publishing Company is the exclusive school and library distributor of Rabbit Ears Books.

Library bound edition 2005.

Copyright © 1995 Rabbit Ears Entertainment, LLC.,
S. Norwalk, Connecticut.

Library of Congress Cataloging-in-Publication Data

Roberts, Tom, 1944-
   Red Riding Hood / collected by the Brothers Grimm ; adapted by Tom Roberts ; illustrated by
Laszlo Kubinyi.
         p. cm.
   "Rabbit Ears books."
   Summary: Retells the adventures of a little girl who meets a wolf in the forest on her way
to visit her grandmother.
   ISBN 1-59197-752-5
   [1. Fairy tales. 2. Folklore—Germany.] I. Kubinyi, Laszlo, 1937- ill. II. Little Red Riding
Hood. English. III. Title.

PZ8.R524Re 2004
398.2—dc22
[E]

                                                                              2004045798

All Rabbit Ears books are reinforced library binding
and manufactured in the United States of America.

Collected by the Brothers Grimm

Adapted by Tom Roberts

Red Riding Hood

Illustrated by Laszlo Kubinyi

Rabbit Ears Books

Red was her favorite color, even though her hair was a deep red and her cheeks most often a cherry red. Her mother tried to convince her to wear other colors. But red it was, even to the name her friends called her: Red. Her real name, truth to tell, was Millicent. But no one ever called her that, and neither shall we.

Red was especially close to her grandmother, who lived a few miles away through a forest lush and deep and dense. Granny was devoted to Red and, as old as she was, visited often. Granny delighted in bringing Red gifts she had made: mittens and slippers and sweaters to wear, cookies and muffins and puddings to eat. But of all of these gifts, Red's favorite was the hooded cape of warm wool woven by her grandmother. Needless to say, the cape was as red as a blushing rose.

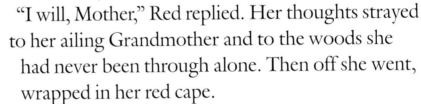

One autumn day, Red's mother told her that Granny was ill, too weak to walk through the woods alone.

"I've readied a basket with bread and cakes for you to take to dear Granny," said her mother. "Go there directly, don't stray from the path, and be home before dark."

Red was always in bed by dusk, so it never occurred to her to be by herself in the woods at night. She ran to get her hooded cape and returned to her mother.

"Remember what I've said," her mother went on, "straight to Granny's, no delay. And mind your manners while you're there."

"I will, Mother," Red replied. Her thoughts strayed to her ailing Grandmother and to the woods she had never been through alone. Then off she went, wrapped in her red cape.

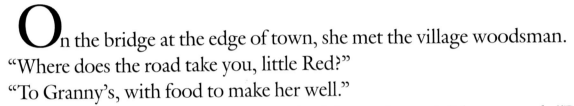

On the bridge at the edge of town, she met the village woodsman.
"Where does the road take you, little Red?"
"To Granny's, with food to make her well."

"Take care you don't leave the path," he warned. "Danger is lurking behind every leaf."

Red nodded and smiled, staring ahead at the towering trees but not really hearing the woodsman's warnings.

Before he could continue, though, she was skipping along the path and into the woods. The woodsman watched her go and wished her well.

Deeper into the woods Red walked, marveling at the magnificent foliage and breathing in the cool, damp air that surrounded her. And always she stayed on the path.

Rounding a bend, she came upon a sharp looking fellow leaning against a tree. He fairly glowed with his silver fur coat and his dark gleaming eyes. He was a wolf and he had been watching her for some time. Now, Red had never met a wolf before nor even heard of one.

"How handsome he is," Red thought, trying not to stare. The wolf looked her over with a steady gaze that tickled her and terrified her all at once.

"What a beautiful cape," purred the wolf. "Blood red, my favorite shade." He smiled. "And what a beautiful girl wearing it."

Red blushed so deeply that it was hard to tell where she left off and her cape began.

"Have we met before?" asked the wolf. "I think not. I surely would remember such a savory rosebud. One with such delicious taste in clothes." The wolf smiled again.

R̲ed smiled back. "Thank you, sir," she whispered, and curtsied as her mother had taught her.

"What is in your basket?" he inquired.

"Bread and cakes to make my Granny well."

"Delicious," smiled the wolf. "But what a long trip for such a tender tulip."

"Oh, no," Red protested, "Granny's house is just past the cypress grove."

The wolf could barely curb his appetite. He was tempted to wolf her down right there. But then he thought to himself, "Why settle for a single course? Why not both? First a bit of dried Granny, aged on the bone, and then this apple dumpling for dessert. He said aloud to her, "You'd best hurry along then. Granny craves a crust of bread and,"

he hesitated, "yearns for your yummy wildflowers."

The color drained from Red's cheeks, though not from her cape. "But I have no wildflowers."

"No wildfl…?" choked the wolf. Red shook her head. He paused. "Perhaps she'll be too tasteful to notice."

A tear welled up in Red's eye.

"Now, now my dumpling, there's no need for that," comforted the wolf. "Look around you. Wildflowers. Wildflowers everywhere, and," he confided, "the farther from the path you go, the more succulent the buds."

"Oh, thank you, sir," Red said. Whatever succulent was, Granny would certainly like it. So off the path she stepped, plucking flower after flower, all the while straying farther into the woods, farther from the path.

The wolf ran straight to Granny's house and knocked on the door. "Who is it?" rasped Granny, unable to pull herself out of bed. Taking a deep breath and putting on his most innocent girlish voice, the wolf replied, "It's Red, Granny. I've brought you luscious bread and cakes to make you well."

"Do you have a cold, my dear?" asked Granny. "You sound so hoarse." The wolf coughed delicately. "Will you let me in?" he asked.

"Just lift the latch and let yourself in, my dear." Lift the latch he did, and in one bound he leapt on Granny, lapped her up, and licked his lips. The wolf had swallowed the sweet old lady in one greedy gulp. "Ahhh," he sighed, sinking back on Granny's pillows. Then, with a plan he'd concocted as he was chatting with Red, he put on Granny's nightcap and went around closing the shutters.

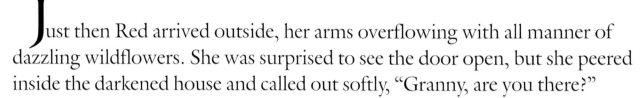

Just then Red arrived outside, her arms overflowing with all manner of dazzling wildflowers. She was surprised to see the door open, but she peered inside the darkened house and called out softly, "Granny, are you there?"

In reply, she heard a deep, but delicate cough.

"Oh my," she thought, "how sick Granny must be."

Feeling frightened, Red approached the bed. Usually a visit to Granny made her happy, but she was uneasy. In the dim light, she saw Granny lying in bed, her nightcap pulled down over her face.

"How odd she looks," thought Red.

The wolf coughed delicately again and pulled the covers up around his chin.

"Why, Granny," said Red, "what big arms you have."

"The better to hug you with," whispered the wolf.

Stepping closer to the bed, Red noticed the wolf's ears peeking through Granny's nightcap.

"Why, Granny," said Red, "what big ears you have."

"The better to hear you with," whispered the wolf.

Still closer, Red saw a familiar but unsettling gleam in Granny's eyes.

"Why, Granny, what big eyes you have."

"The better to see you with," whispered the wolf. By now, Red was close enough to see the wolf's magnificent molars as he spoke.

"Why, Granny, what big teeth you have."

"The better to eat you with," roared the wolf. And in one bound he leapt on Red, lapped her up, and licked his lips. He had swallowed the lovable little girl in one resounding gulp.

"Ahh," he sighed, rubbing his swollen stomach and sinking back into Granny's pillows. In no time at all, he was sound asleep and snoring like a swarm of hornets.

Just then, the village woodsman happened to be hiking by. He heard the dreadful droning sound from inside Granny's house and saw the open door. Remembering Red's visit, he rushed inside and found the slumbering wolf in Granny's nightclothes. Now the woodsman could tell a weak old woman from a wicked wolf. So he raised his axe over his head, intending to do away with this vicious outlaw in Granny garb. Suddenly, he noticed the wolf's distended stomach. It was twitching and twirling as though there were something inside. Or someone.

The woodsman put down his axe, took out his knife and carefully slit open the wolf's stomach. As he did so, he saw the familiar red cape appear deep inside the wolf. He reached in and pulled Red out.

"Eccch!" sputtered Red. "It's dark and slimy in there."

The woodsman comforted her.

"You mustn't stop now," she cried. "Granny's still in there."

So the woodsman cut some more and soon he pulled Granny out. She was alive !

Red helped the woodsman gather several heavy stones and he stuffed them into the wolf's stomach. When the wolf awoke, he tried to run away but all he could manage was to drag himself out the door.

Red stayed with Granny a few days and nursed her back to health. Then the woodsman, wearing his new silver fur coat, escorted Red back home. And she has never to this day wandered from the path again.